D1388898

The Giant's Necklace

Books by the same author

Didn't We Have a Lovely Time!

Half a Man

Homecoming

I Believe in Unicorns

The Kites are Flying!

Meeting Cézanne

The Mozart Question

My Father Is a Polar Bear

This Morning I Met a Whale

Beowulf

Hansel and Gretel

The Pied Piper of Hamelin

Sir Gawain and the Green Knight

Essays and stories

Singing for Mrs Pettigrew: A Story-maker's Journey

Such Stuff: A Story-maker's Inspiration

MICHAEL MORPURGO

The Giant's Necklace

illustrated by Briony May Smith

WALKER
BOOKS

First published 1982 in *The White Horse of Zennor and Other Stories*

This edition published 2016 by
Walker Books Ltd, 87 Vauxhall Walk, London SE11 5HJ

2 4 6 8 10 9 7 5 3 1

This book has been typeset in Bembo

Printed in China

British Library Cataloguing in Publication Data:
a catalogue record for this book is available from the British Library

ISBN 978-1-4063-5712-7   (hardback)
ISBN 978-1-4063-7626-5   (Scholastic paperback)

www.walker.co.uk

In memory of two remarkable ancestors:
James Dunn, top Cornish smuggler and Methodist minister,
and John Wesley, top preacher – in Cornwall and all over –
both of whom walked this way
M.M.

For Laura
B.M.S.

The necklace stretched from one end of the
kitchen table to the other, around the sugar
bowl at the far end and back again, stopping
only a few inches short of the toaster. The discovery on
the beach of a length of abandoned fishing line draped
with seaweed had first suggested the idea to Cherry; and
every day of the holiday since then had been spent in

one single-minded pursuit, the creation of a necklace of glistening pink cowrie shells. She had sworn to herself and to everyone else that the necklace would not be complete until it reached the toaster; and when Cherry vowed she would do something, she invariably did it.

Cherry was the youngest in a family of older brothers, four of them, who had teased her relentlessly since the day she was born, eleven years before. She referred to them as "the four mistakes", for it was a family joke that each son had been an attempt to produce a daughter. To their huge delight Cherry reacted passionately to any slight or insult whether intended or not. Their particular targets were her size, which was diminutive compared with theirs, her dark flashing eyes that could wither with one scornful look, but above all her ever increasing femininity. Although the teasing was interminable it was

rarely hurtful, nor was it intended to be, for her brothers
adored her; and she knew it.

Cherry was poring over her necklace, still in her
dressing gown. Breakfast had just been cleared away and
she was alone with her mother. She fingered the shells
lightly, turning them gently until the entire
necklace lay flat with the rounded pink
of the shells all uppermost. Then she
bent down and breathed on each of
them in turn, polishing them carefully with a napkin.

"There's still the sea in them,"
she said to no one in particular.
"You can still smell it, and
I washed them and washed them,
you know."

"You've only got today, Cherry," said her mother, coming over to the table and putting an arm around her. "Just today, that's all. We're off back home tomorrow morning first thing. Why don't you call it a day, dear? You've been at it every day – you must be tired of it by now. There's no need to go on, you know. We all think it's a fine necklace and quite long enough. It's long enough surely?"

Cherry shook her head slowly. "Nope," she said. "Only that little bit left to do and then it's finished."

"But they'll take hours to collect, dear," her mother said weakly, recognizing and at the same time respecting her daughter's persistence.

"Only a few hours," said Cherry, bending over, her brows furrowing critically as she inspected a flaw in one of her shells, "that's all it'll take. D'you know, there are five thousand, three hundred and twenty-five shells in my necklace already? I counted them, so I know."

"Isn't that enough?" her mother said desperately.

"Nope," said Cherry. "I said I'd reach the toaster, and I'm going to reach the toaster."

Her mother turned away to continue the drying up.

"Well, I can't spend all day on the beach today, Cherry," she said. "If you haven't finished by the time we come away I'll have to leave you there. We've got to pack up and tidy the house – there'll be no time in the morning."

"I'll be all right," said Cherry, cocking her head on one side to view the necklace from a different angle. "There's never been a necklace like this before, not in all the world. I'm sure there hasn't." And then: "You can leave me there, Mum, and I'll walk back. It's only a mile or so along the cliff path and half a mile back across the fields. I've done it before on my own. It's not far."

There was a thundering on the stairs and a sudden rude invasion of the kitchen. Cherry was surrounded by her four brothers, who leant over the table in mock appreciation of her necklace.

"Ooh, pretty."

"Do they come in other colours? I mean, pink's not my colour."

"Bit big though, isn't it?" said one of them – she didn't know which and it didn't matter. He went on: "I mean it's

a bit big for a necklace." War had been declared again, and Cherry responded predictably.

"That depends," she said calmly, shrugging her shoulders because she knew that would irritate them.

"On what does it depend?" said her eldest brother pompously.

"On who's going to wear it of course, ninny," she said swiftly.

"Well, who is going to wear it?" he replied.

"It's for a giant," she said, her voice full of serious innocence. "It's a giant's necklace, and it's still not big enough."

It was the perfect answer, an answer she knew would

send her brothers into fits of hysterical hilarity. She loved to make them laugh at her and could do it at the drop of a hat. Of course she no more believed in giants than they did, but if it tickled them pink to believe she did, then why not pretend?

She turned on them, fists flailing, and chased them back up the stairs, her eyes burning with simulated fury. "Just cos you don't believe in anything 'cept motorbikes and football and all that rubbish, just cos you're great big, fat, ignorant pigs..." She hurled insults up the stairs after them and the worse they became the more they loved it.

Boat Cove just below Zennor Head was the beach they had found and occupied. Every year for as long as Cherry could remember they had rented the same granite cottage, set back in the fields below the Eagle's Nest, and every year they came to the same beach because no one else did. In two weeks not another soul had ventured down the winding track through the bracken from the coastal path. It was a long climb down and a very

much longer one up. The beach itself was almost hidden from the path that ran along the cliff top a hundred feet above. It was private and perfect and theirs. The boys swam in amongst the rocks, diving and snorkelling for hours on end. Her mother and father would sit side by side on stripy deckchairs. She would read endlessly and he would close his eyes against the sun and dream for hours on end.

Cherry moved away from her family and clambered over the rocks to a narrow strip of sand in the cove beyond the rocks, and here it was that she mined for the cowrie shells. In the gritty sand under the cliff face she had found a particularly rich deposit, so they were not hard to find; but she was looking for pink cowrie shells of a uniform length, colour and shape – and that was what took the time. Occasionally the boys would swim around the rocks and in to her little beach, emerging from the sea all goggled and flippered to mock her. But as she paid them little attention they soon tired and went away again. She knew time was running short.

This was her very last chance to find enough shells to complete the giant's necklace, and it had to be done.

The sea was calmer that day than she had ever seen it. The heat beat down from a windless, cloudless sky; even the gulls and kittiwakes seemed to be silenced by the sun. Cherry searched on, stopping only for a picnic lunch of pasties and tomatoes with the family before returning at once to her shells.

In the end the heat proved too much for her mother and father, who left the beach earlier than usual in mid-afternoon to begin to tidy up the cottage. The boys soon followed because they had tired of finding miniature crabs and seaweed instead of the sunken wrecks and treasure they had been seeking, so by teatime Cherry was left on her own on the beach with strict instructions not to bathe alone and to be back well before dark. She had calculated she needed one hundred and fifty more cowrie shells, and so far she had found only eighty. She would be back, she

insisted, when she had finished collecting enough shells and not before.

Had she not been so immersed in her search, sifting the shells through her fingers, she would have noticed the dark grey bank of cloud rolling in from the Atlantic. She would have noticed the white horses gathering out at sea and the tide moving remorselessly in to cover the rocks between her and Boat Cove. When the clouds cut off the warmth from the sun as evening came on and the sea turned grey, she shivered with cold and slipped

on her jersey and jeans. She did look up then and saw that the sea was angry, but she saw no threat in that and did not look back over her shoulder towards Boat Cove. She was aware that time was running short so she went down on her knees again and dug feverishly in the sand. There were still thirty shells to collect and she was not going home without them.

It was the baleful sound of a foghorn somewhere out at sea beyond Gunnards Head that at last forced Cherry to consider her own predicament. Only then did she take some account of the incoming tide. She looked for the rocks she would have to clamber over

to reach Boat Cove again and the winding track that would take her up to the cliff path and safety, but they were gone. Where they should have been, the sea was already driving in against the cliff face. She was cut off. For many moments Cherry stared in disbelief and wondered if her memory was deceiving her, until the sea, sucked back into the Atlantic for a brief moment,

revealed the rocks that marked her route back to Boat Cove. Then she realized at last that the sea had undergone a grim metamorphosis. In a confusion of wonder and fear she looked out to sea at the heaving ocean that moved in towards her, seeing it now as a writhing grey monster breathing its fury on the rocks with every pounding wave.

Still Cherry did not forget her shells, but wrapping them inside her towel she tucked them into her jersey and waded out through the surf towards the rocks. If she timed it right, she reasoned, she could scramble back over them and into the cove as the surf retreated. And she reached the first of the rocks without too much difficulty; the sea here seemed to be protected from the force of the ocean by the rocks further out. Holding fast to the first rock she came to, and with the sea up around her waist, she waited for the next incoming wave to break and retreat. The wave was unexpectedly impotent and fell limply on the rocks around her. She knew her moment had come and took it. She was not to know that piling up far out at sea was the first of the giant storm waves that had gathered several hundred miles out in the Atlantic, bringing with it all the momentum and violence of the deep ocean.

The rocks were slippery underfoot and more than once Cherry slipped down into seething white rock pools where she had played so often when the tide was out. But she struggled on until finally she had climbed high enough to be able to see the thin strip of sand that was all that was left of Boat Cove. It was only a few yards away, so close. Until now she had been crying involuntarily; but now, as she recognized the little path up through the bracken, her heart was lifted with hope and anticipation. She knew that the worst was over, that if the sea would only hold back she would reach the sanctuary of the cove. She turned and looked behind her to see how far away the next wave was, just to reassure herself that she had enough time. But the great surge of green water was on her before she could register either disappointment or fear. She was hurled back against the rock below her and covered at once by the sea. She was conscious as she went down that she was drowning, but she still clutched her shells against her chest and was glad she had enough of them at last to finish the giant's necklace. Those were her last thinking thoughts before the sea took her away.

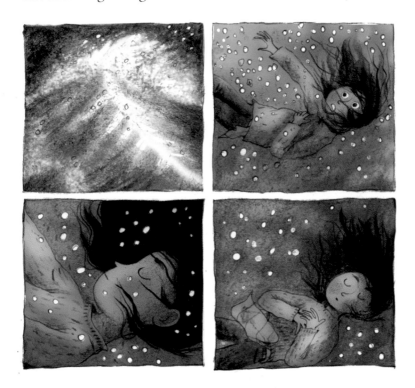

*   *   *

Cherry lay on her side where the tide had lifted her and coughed until her lungs were clear. She woke as the sea came in once again and frothed around her legs. She rolled over on her back, feeling the salt spray on her face, and saw that it was night. The sky above her was dashed with stars and the moon rode through the clouds.

She scrambled to her feet, one hand still holding her precious shells close to her. Instinctively she backed away from the sea and looked around her. With growing dismay she saw that she had been thrown back on the wrong side of the rocks, that she was not in Boat Cove. The tide had left only a few feet of sand and rock between her and the cliff face. There was no way back through the sea to safety.

She turned round to face the cliff that she realized would be her last hope, for she remembered that this little beach vanished completely at high tide. If she stayed where she was she would surely be swept away again and this time she might not be so fortunate. But the cold seemed to have calmed her and she reasoned more deliberately now, wondering why she had not tried climbing the cliff before. She had hurried into her first attempt at escape and it had very nearly cost her her life. She would wait this time until the sea forced her up the cliff. Perhaps the tide would not come in that far. Perhaps they would be looking for her by now. It was dark. Surely they would be searching. Surely they must find her soon. After all, they knew where she was. Yes, she thought, best just to wait and hope.

She settled down on a ledge of rock that was the

first step up onto the cliff face, drew her knees up to her chin to keep out the chill and waited. She watched as the sea crept ever closer, each wave lashing her with spray and eating away gradually at the beach. She closed her eyes and prayed, hoping against hope that when she opened them the sea would be retreating. But her prayers went unanswered and the sea came in to cover the beach. Once or twice she thought she heard voices above her on the cliff path, but when she called out no one came. She continued to shout for help every few minutes, forgetting it was futile against the continuous roar and hiss of the waves. A pair of raucous white gulls flew down from the cliffs to investigate her and she called to them for help, but they did not seem to understand and wheeled away into the night.

She stayed sitting on her rock until the waves threatened

to dislodge her and then reluctantly she began her climb. She would go as far as she needed to and no further. She had scanned the first few feet above for footholds and it did look quite a simple climb to begin with, and so it proved. But her hands were numbed with cold and her legs began to tremble with the strain almost at once. She could see that the ledge she had now reached was the last deep one visible on the cliff face. The shells in her jersey were restricting her freedom of movement, so she decided she would leave them there. Wrapped tight in the towel they would be quite safe. She took the soaking bundle out of her jersey and placed it carefully against the rock face on the ledge beside her, pushing it in as far as it would go. "I'll be back for you," she said, and reached up for the next lip of rock. Just below her the sea crashed against the cliff as if it wanted to suck her from the rock face and claim her

once again. Cherry determined not to look down but to concentrate on the climb.

She imagined at first that the glow of light above her was from a torch, and she shouted and screamed until she was weak from the effort of it. But although no answering call came from the night, the light remained, a pale beckoning light whose source now seemed to her wider perhaps than that of a torch. With renewed hope that had

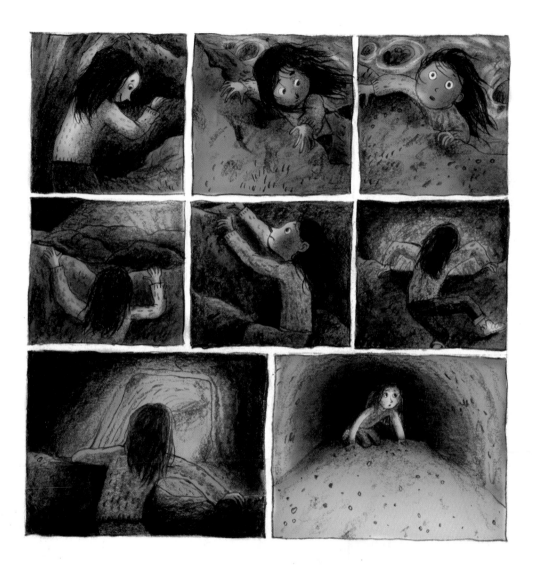

rekindled her strength and her courage, Cherry inched her way up the cliff towards the light until she found herself at the entrance to a narrow cave that was filled with a flickering yellow light like that of a candle shaken by the wind. She hauled herself up into the mouth of the cave and sat down exhausted, looking back down at the furious sea frothing beneath her. Relief and joy surged within her and she laughed aloud in triumph. She was safe and she had defied the sea and won. Her one regret was that she had had to leave her cowrie shells behind on the ledge. They were high enough she thought to escape the sea. She would fetch them tomorrow after the tide had gone down again.

For the first time now she began to think of her family and how worried they would be, but the thought of walking in through the front door all dripping and dramatic made her almost choke with excitement.

As she reached forward to brush a sharp stone from the sole of her foot, Cherry noticed that the narrow entrance to the cave was half sealed in. She ran her fingers over the stones and cement to make sure, for the light was poor. It was at that moment that she recognized exactly where she was. She recalled now the giant fledgling cuckoo one of her brothers had spotted being fed by a tiny rock pipit earlier in the holidays, how they had quarrelled over the binoculars and how when she finally usurped them and made her escape across the rocks she had found the cuckoo perched at the entrance to a narrow cave some way up the cliff face from the beach.

She had asked then about the man-made walling, and her father had told her of the old tin mines whose lodes and adits criss-crossed the entire coastal area around Zennor. This one, he said, might have been the mine they called Wheel North Grylls, and he thought the adit must have been walled up to prevent the seas from entering the mine in a storm. It was said there had been an accident in the mine only a few years after it was opened, over a hundred years before, and that the mine had had to close soon after when the mine owners ran out of money to make the necessary repairs. The entire story came back to her now, and she wondered where the cuckoo was and whether the rock pipit had died with the effort of keeping the fledgling alive. Tin mines, she thought, lead to the surface, and the way home. That thought and her natural inquisitiveness about the source of light persuaded her to her feet and into the tunnel.

The adit became narrower and lower as she crept forward, so she had to go down on her hands and knees and sometimes flat on her stomach. Although she was now out of the wind, it seemed colder. She felt she was moving downwards for

a minute or two, for the blood was coming to her head and her weight was heavy on her hands. Then, quite suddenly, she found the ground levelling out and saw a large tunnel ahead of her. There was no doubt as to which way she should turn, for one way the tunnel was black and the other way was lighted with candles that lined the lode wall as far as she could see. She called out, "Anyone there? Anyone there?" and paused to listen for the reply; but all she could hear now was the

muffled roar of the sea and the continuous echoing of dripping water.

The tunnel widened now and she could walk upright again; but her feet hurt against the stone and so she moved slowly, feeling her way gently with each foot. She had gone only a short distance when she heard the tapping for the first time, distinct and rhythmic, a sound that was instantly recognizable as hammering. It became sharper and noticeably more metallic as she moved up the tunnel. She could hear the distant murmur of voices and the sound of falling stone. Even before she came out of the tunnel and into the vast cave she knew she had happened upon a working mine.

The cave was dark in all but one corner and here she could see two men bending to their work, their backs towards her. One of them was inspecting the rock face closely whilst the other swung his hammer with controlled power, pausing only to spit on his hands from time to time. They wore round hats with turned-up brims that served also as candlesticks, for a lighted candle was fixed

to each, the light dancing with the shadows along the cave walls as they worked.

Cherry watched for some moments until she made up her mind what to do. She longed to rush up to them and tell of her escape and to ask them to take her to the surface, but a certain shyness overcame her and she held back. Her chance to interrupt came when they sat down against the rock face and opened their canteens. She was in the shadows and they still could not see her.

"Tea looks cold again," one of them said gruffly. "'Tis always cold. I'm sure she makes it wi' cold water."

"Oh, stop your moaning, Father," said the other, a

younger voice, Cherry felt. "She does her best. She's five little ones to look after and precious little to do it on. She does her best. You mustn't keep on at her so. It upsets her. She does her best."

"So she does, lad, so she does. And so for that matter do I, but that don't stop her moaning at me and it'll not stop me moaning at her. If we didn't moan at each other, lad, we'd have precious little else to talk about, and that's a fact. She expects it of me, lad, and I expects it of her."

"Excuse me," Cherry said tentatively. She felt she had eavesdropped for long enough. She approached them slowly. "Excuse me, but I've got a bit lost. I climbed the cliff, you see, cos I was cut off from the cove. I was trying to get back, but I couldn't and I saw this light and so I climbed up. I want to get home and I wondered if you could help me get to the top?"

"Top?" said the older one, peering into the dark. "Come closer, lad, where we can see you."

"She's not a lad, Father. Are you blind? Can you not see 'tis a filly. 'Tis a young filly, all wet through from the sea. Come," the young man said, standing up and beckoning Cherry in. "Don't be afeared, little girl, we shan't harm you. Come on, you can have some of my tea if you like."

They spoke their words in a manner Cherry had never heard before. It was not the usual Cornish burr, but

heavier and rougher in tone and somehow old-fashioned. There were so many questions in her mind.

"But I thought the mine was closed a hundred years ago," she said nervously. "That's what I was told, anyway."

"Well, you was told wrong," said the old man, whom Cherry could see more clearly now under his candle. His eyes were white and set far back in his head, unnaturally so, she thought, and his lips and mouth seemed a vivid red in the candlelight.

"Closed, closed indeed; does it look closed to you? D'you think we're digging for worms? Over four thousand tons of tin last year and nine thousand of copper ore, and you ask is the mine closed? Over twenty fathoms below the sea this mine goes. We'll dig right out under the ocean, most of the way to 'Merica, afore we close down this mine."

He spoke passionately now, almost angrily, so that Cherry felt she had offended him.

"Hush, Father," said the young man, taking off his jacket and wrapping it around Cherry's shoulders.

"She doesn't want to hear all about that. She's cold and wet. Can't you see? Now, let's make a little fire to warm her through. She's shivered right through to her bones. You can see she is."

"They all are," said the old tinner, pulling himself to his feet. "They all are." And he shuffled past her into the dark. "I'll fetch the wood," he muttered, and then added, "for all the good it'll do."

"What does he mean?" Cherry asked the young man, for whom she felt an instant liking. "What did he mean by that?"

"Oh, pay him no heed, little girl," he said. "He's an old man now and tired of the mine. We're both tired of it, but we're proud of it, see, and we've nowhere else to go, nothing else to do."

He had a kind voice that was reassuring to Cherry.

He seemed somehow to know the questions she wanted to ask, for he answered them now without her ever asking.

"Sit down by me while you listen, girl," he said. "Father will make a fire to warm you and I shall tell you how we come to be here. You won't be afeared now, will you?"

Cherry looked up into his face, which was younger than she had expected from his voice; but like his father's, the eyes seemed sad and deep-set, yet they smiled at her gently and she smiled back.

"That's my girl. It was a new mine, this; promising, everyone said. The best tin in Cornwall and that means the best tin in the world. Eighteen sixty-five it started up and they were looking for tinners, and so Father found a cottage down by Treveal and came to work here. I was already fourteen, so I joined him down the mine. We prospered and the mine prospered, to start with. Mother and the little children had full bellies and there was talk of sinking a fresh shaft. Times were good and promised to be better."

Cherry sat transfixed as the story of the disaster unfolded. She heard how they had been trapped by a fall of rock, about how they had worked to pull them away, but behind every rock was another rock and another rock. She heard how they had never even heard any sound of rescue. They had died, he said, in two days or so because the air was bad and because there was too little of it.

"Father has never accepted it; he still thinks he's alive, that he goes home to Mother and the little children each evening. But he's dead, just like me. I can't tell him though, for he'd not understand and it would break his heart if he ever knew."

"So you aren't real," said Cherry, trying to grasp the implications of his story. "So I'm just imagining all this. You're just a dream."

"No dream, my girl," said the young man, laughing out loud. "No more'n we're imagining you. We're real right enough, but we're dead and have been for a hundred years and more. Ghosts, spirits, that's what living folk call us. Come to think of it, that's what *I* called us when I was alive."

Cherry was on her feet suddenly and backing away.

"No need to be afeared, little girl," said the young

man, holding out his hand towards her. "We won't harm you. No one can harm you, not now. Look, he's started the fire already. Come over and warm yourself. Come, it'll be all right, girl. We'll look after you. We'll help you."

"But I want to go home," Cherry said, feeling the panic rising to her voice and trying to control it. "I know you're kind, but I want to go home. My mother will be worried about me. They'll be out looking for me. Your light saved my life and I want to thank you. But I must go, else they'll worry themselves sick, I know they will."

"You going back home?" the young man asked, and then he nodded. "I s'pose you'll want to see your family again."

"Course I am," said Cherry, perplexed by the question. "Course I do."

"'Tis a pity," he said sadly. "Everyone passes through and no one stays. They all want to go home, but then so do I. You'll want me to guide you to the surface, I s'pose."

"I'm not the first then?" Cherry said. "There's been others climb up into the mine to escape from the sea? You've saved lots of people."

"A few," said the tinner, nodding. "A few."

"You're a kind person," Cherry said, warming to the sadness in the young man's voice. "I never thought ghosts would be kind."

"We're just people, people who've passed on," replied the young man, taking her elbow and leading her towards the fire. "There's nice people and there's nasty people. It's the same if you're alive or if you're dead. You're a nice person, I can tell that, even though I haven't known you for long. I'm sad because I should like to be alive again

with my friends and go rabbiting or blackberrying up by the chapel near Treveal like I used to. The sun always seemed to be shining then. After it happened I used to go up to the surface often and move amongst the people in the village. I went to see my family, but if I spoke to them they never seemed to hear me, and of course they can't see you. You can see them, but they can't see you. That's the worst of it. So I don't go up much now, just to

collect wood for the fire and a bit of food now and then. I stay down here with Father in the mine and we work away day after day, and from time to time someone like you comes up the tunnel from the sea and lightens our darkness. I shall be sad when you go."

The old man was hunched over the fire rubbing his hands and holding them out over the heat.

"Not often we have a fire," he said, his voice more sprightly now. "Only on special occasions. Birthdays, of course, we always have a fire on birthdays back at the cottage. Martha's next. You don't know her; she's my only daughter – she'll be eight on September 10th. She's been poorly, you know – her lungs, that's what the doctor said." He sighed deeply. "'Tis dreadful damp in the cottage. 'Tis well nigh impossible to keep it out." There was a tremor in the old man's voice that betrayed his emotion. He looked up at Cherry and she could see the tears in his eyes. "She looks a bit like you, my dear, raven-haired and as pretty as a picture; but not so tall, not so tall. Come in closer, my dear, you'll be warmer that way."

Cherry sat with them by the fire till it died away to nothing. She longed to go, to get home amongst the living, but the old man talked on of his family and their little one-room cottage with a ladder to the bedroom where they all huddled together for warmth, of his friends that used to meet in the Tinners' Arms every evening. There were tales of wrecking and smuggling, and all the while the young man sat silent until there was a lull in the story.

"Father," he said. "I think our little friend would like to go home now. Shall I take her up as I usually do?"

The old man nodded and waved his hand in dismissal.

"Come back and see us sometime, if you've a mind to," he said, and then put his face in his hands.

"Goodbye," said Cherry. "Thank you for the fire and for helping me. I won't forget you."

But the old man never replied.

The journey through the mine was long and difficult. She held fast to the young tinner's waist as they walked silently through the dark tunnels, stopping every now and then to climb a ladder to the lode above until finally they could look up the shaft above them and see the daylight.

"It's dawn," said the young man, looking up.

"I'll be back in time for breakfast," said Cherry, setting her foot on the ladder.

"You'll remember me?" the young tinner asked, and Cherry nodded, unable to speak. She felt a strange affinity with him and his father. "And if you should ever need me, come back again. You may need me and I shall be here. I go nowhere else."

"Thank you," said Cherry. "I won't forget. I doubt anyone is going to believe me when I tell them about you. No one believes in ghosts, not up there."

"I doubt it too. Be happy, little friend," he said. And he was gone, back into the tunnel. Cherry waited until the light from the candle in his hat had vanished and then turned eagerly to the ladder and began to climb up towards the light.

She found herself in a place she knew well, high on
the moor by Zennor Quoit. She stood by the ruined
mine workings and looked down at the sleeping village
shrouded in mist, and the calm blue sea beyond. The
storm had passed and there was scarcely a breath of wind

even on the moor. It was only ten minutes' walk down through the bracken, across the road by the Eagle's Nest and down the farm track to the cottage where her family would be waiting. She began to run, but her clothes were still heavy and wet and she was soon reduced to a fast walk. All the while she was determining where she would begin her story, wondering how much they would believe. At the top of the lane she stopped to consider how best to make her entrance. Should she ring the bell and be found standing there, or should she just walk in and surprise them there at breakfast? She longed to see the joy on their faces, to feel the warmth of their arms around her and to bask once again in their affection.

She saw as she came round the corner by the cottage that there was a long blue Land Rover parked in the lane bristling with aerials. *Coastguard*, she read on the side.

As she came down the steps she noticed that the back door of the cottage was open and she could hear voices inside. She stole in on tiptoe. The kitchen was full of uniformed men drinking tea, and around the table sat her family, dejection and despair etched on every face. They hadn't seen her yet. One of the uniformed men had put down his cup and was speaking. His voice was low and hushed.

"You're sure the towel is hers, no doubts about it?"

Cherry's mother shook her head.

"It's her towel," she said quietly, "and they are her shells. She must have put them up there, it must have been the last thing she did."

Cherry saw her shells spread out on the open towel and stifled a shout of joy.

"We have to say," he went on. "We have to say then, most regrettably, that the chances of finding your daughter alive now are very slim. It seems she must have tried to

climb the cliff to escape the heavy seas and fallen in. We've scoured the cliff top for miles in both directions and covered the entire beach, and there's no sign of her. She must have been washed out to sea. We must conclude that she is missing, and we have to presume that she is drowned."

Cherry could listen no longer but burst into the room, shouting.

"I'm home, I'm home. Look at me, I'm not drowned at all. I'm here! I'm home!"

The tears were running down her face.

But no one in the room even turned to look in her direction. Her brothers cried openly, one of them clutching the giant's necklace.

"But it's me!" she shouted again. "Me, can't you see? It's me and I've come back. I'm all right. Look at me."

But no one did, and no one heard.

The giant's necklace lay spread out on the table.

"So she'll never finish it after all," said her mother softly. "Poor Cherry. Poor dear Cherry."

And in that one moment Cherry knew and understood that she was right, that she would never finish her necklace, that she belonged no longer with the living but had passed on beyond.